W9-BNM-607

PIGS

Story by Robert Munsch
Art by Michael Martchenko

Annick Press Ltd.
Toronto • New York • Vancouver

Thirteenth printing, July 1999

Annick Press Ltd.

Annick Press gratefully acknowledges the support of the
Canada Council and the Ontario Arts Council.

Cataloguing in Publication Data
  Munsch, Robert N., 1945–
    Pigs

  (Munsch for kids)
  ISBN 1-55037-039-1 (bound) ISBN 1-55037-038-3 (pbk.)

  I. Martchenko, Michael. II. Title. III. Series
  Munsch, Robert N., 1945- . Munsch for kids.

  PS8576.U58P53 1989   jC813'.54 C89-093009-0
  PZ7.M86Pi 1989

Distributed in Canada by:
Firefly Books Ltd.
3680 Victoria Park Avenue
Willowdale, ON
M2H 3K1

Published in the U.S.A. by Annick Press (U.S.) Ltd.
Distributed in the U.S.A. by:
Firefly Books (U.S.) Inc.
P.O. Box 1338
Ellicott Station
Buffalo, NY 14205

Printed and bound in Canada by
Metropole Litho Inc., Montréal, Québec.

Megan's father asked her to feed the pigs on her way to school. He said, "Megan, please feed the pigs, but don't open the gate. Pigs are smarter than you think. Don't open the gate."

"Right," said Megan. "I will not open the gate. Not me. No sir. No, no, no, no, no."

So Megan went to the pig pen. She looked at the pigs. The pigs looked at Megan.

Megan said, "These are the dumbest looking animals I have ever seen. They stand there like lumps on a bump. They wouldn't do anything if I did open the gate." So Megan opened the gate just a little bit. The pigs stood there and looked at Megan. They didn't do anything.

Megan said, "These are the dumbest looking animals I have ever seen. They stand there like lumps on a bump. They wouldn't even go out the door if the house was on fire." So Megan opened the gate a little bit more. The pigs stood there and looked at Megan. They didn't do anything.

Then Megan yelled, "HEY YOU DUMB PIGS!"
The pigs jumped up and ran right over Megan,
WAP—WAP—WAP—WAP—WAP,
and out the gate.

When Megan got up she couldn't see the pigs anywhere. She said, "Uh-Oh, I am in bad trouble. Maybe pigs are not so dumb after all." Then she went to tell her father the bad news. When she got to the house Megan heard a noise coming from the kitchen. It went, "OINK, OINK, OINK."

"That doesn't sound like my mother. That doesn't sound like my father. That sounds like pigs."

She looked in the window. There was her father sitting at the breakfast table. A pig was drinking his coffee. A pig was eating his newspaper. And a pig was peeing on his shoe. "Megan," yelled her father, "you opened the gate. Get these pigs out of here."

Megan opened the front door a little bit. The pigs stood and looked at Megan. Finally Megan opened the front door all the way and yelled, "HEY YOU DUMB PIGS." The pigs jumped up and ran right over Megan, WAP—WAP—WAP—WAP—WAP, and out the door.

Megan ran outside, chased all the pigs into the pig pen and shut the gate. Then she looked at the pigs and said, "You are still dumb, like lumps on a bump." Then she ran off to school. Just as she was about to open the front door, she heard a sound. OINK, OINK, OINK.

She said, "That doesn't sound like my teacher. That doesn't sound like the principal. That sounds like pigs."

Megan looked in the principal's window. There was a pig drinking the principal's coffee. A pig was eating the principal's newspaper. And a pig was peeing on the principal's shoe. The principal yelled, "Megan, get these pigs out of here!"

Megan opened the front door of the school a little bit. The pigs didn't do anything. She opened it a little bit more. The pigs still didn't do anything. She opened the door all the way and yelled, "HEY YOU DUMB PIGS." The pigs jumped up and ran right over Megan,
WAP—WAP—WAP—WAP—WAP,
and out the door.

Megan went into the school. She sat down at the desk and said, "That's that! I finally got rid of all the pigs." Then she heard a noise. OINK OINK OINK. Megan opened her desk and there was a new baby pig. The teacher said, "Megan! Get that dumb pig out of here!"

Megan said, "Dumb? Who ever said pigs were dumb? Pigs are smart. I am going to keep it for a pet."

At the end of the day the school bus finally came. Megan walked up to the door, then heard something say, "OINK, OINK, OINK."

Megan said, "That doesn't sound like the bus driver. That sounds like a pig." She climbed up the stairs and looked in the bus. There was a pig driving the bus, pigs eating the seats and pigs lying in the aisle.

A pig shut the door and drove the bus down
the road.

It drove the bus all the way to Megan's farm,
through the barnyard and
right into the pig pen.

Megan got out of the bus, walked across the barnyard and marched into the kitchen. She said, "The pigs are all back in the pig pen. They came back by themselves. Pigs are smarter than you think."

And Megan never let out any more animals.

At least not any more pigs.

Other books in the Munsch for Kids series:

The Dark
Mud Puddle
The Paper Bag Princess
The Boy in the Drawer
Jonathan Cleaned Up, Then He Heard a Sound
Murmel Murmel Murmel
Millicent and the Wind
Mortimer
The Fire Station
Angela's Airplane
David's Father
Thomas' Snowsuit
50 Below Zero
I Have to Go!
Moira's Birthday
A Promise is a Promise
Something Good
Show and Tell
Purple, Green and Yellow
Wait and See
Where is Gah-Ning?
From Far Away
Stephanie's Ponytail
Munschworks
Munschworks 2

Many Munsch titles are available in French and/or
Spanish. Please contact your favourite supplier.